CINDERELLA PENGUIN

or, *The Little Glass Flipper*

To Derek

ISBN 0-590-67727-6

Copyright © 1992 by Janet Perlman.
All rights reserved. Published by Scholastic Inc., 555 Broadway,
New York, NY 10012, by arrangement with Puffin Books, a division of
Penguin Books USA Inc. Based on the Janet Perlman animated film
The Tender Tale of Cinderella Penguin, copyright © 1982 by
National Film Board of Canada.

25 24 23 22   6/0

Printed in the U.S.A.   40

First Scholastic printing, January 1996

CINDERELLA PENGUIN

OR, *The Little Glass Flipper*

RETOLD AND ILLUSTRATED BY

JANET PERLMAN

SCHOLASTIC INC.

New York Toronto London Auckland Sydney

THERE once was a young penguin named Cinderella, who lived in a faraway land with her stepmother and two stepsisters. Cinderella was a kind and gentle penguin, but her stepsisters were selfish and vain. Cinderella did all the chores. She even had to pick up after her stepsisters, while they never had to do a thing.

The sisters wore the finest of clothes and slept in large,
cozy feather beds with silk sheets and fluffy pillows.

Poor Cinderella wore nothing but worn-out tatters and
slept in the cold, stone cellar, up on a small shelf beside some
old tin plates.

One day it was announced that the Penguin Prince was giving a costume ball. The stepsisters and their mother received an invitation. Cinderella wanted to go, too, but they just laughed at her.

"The Prince would never want to meet a shabby cinderblock like you!"

For weeks the house was filled with talk of the ball. The sisters had costumes made from the finest fabrics. They ate only the tiniest meals so they could have the tiniest waists, and they were always in front of the mirror, posing and practising their curtsies.

Finally the night of the ball arrived. Cinderella rushed about, ironing her stepsisters' costumes and helping them dress. Then, without a thank you or goodbye, the carriage swept the stepmother and stepsisters off to the ball.

Cinderella burst into tears; she felt so alone and unhappy.

Suddenly, in a glow of blue light, the Great Fairy Penguin appeared before her.

"Why are you crying, Cinderella? Do you want to go to the ball?" she asked.

Cinderella blinked back her tears. "Oh yes, more than anything!"

"Then you shall!"

"First," said the Fairy Penguin, "you must fetch me a pumpkin from the garden."

Cinderella didn't know how a pumpkin could help her get to the ball, but she quickly brought her the best one she could find.

The Fairy gave it a firm tap with her wand, and it magically turned into a beautiful golden carriage.

Then the Great Fairy Penguin went into the kitchen and found six mice carrying a huge chunk of cheese. With a tap of her wand, they turned into a handsome team of six horses. She turned the cheese into a fat coachman in uniform. They all marched out the door and took their places, as if it were the most natural thing to do.

"Now you can go to the ball! Are you happy, Cinderella?" asked the Fairy.

"Oh, yes," said Cinderella. But then she looked sadly down at her ragged clothes.

"Oh, I almost forgot!" said the Fairy.

And with a tap of her wand, Cinderella Penguin's rags became a beautiful gown with gold trimming and a real gold tiara. On her feet were a pair of glass flippers, the prettiest and most delicate that Cinderella had ever seen.

"Now, one last thing," said the Great Fairy Penguin. "The
magic spell ends at the stroke of midnight. The carriage will
turn back into a pumpkin, the horses back into mice, the
coachman into cheese, and you'll again be dressed in rags. So
you must leave the ball before midnight."

Cinderella promised to remember. Then, waving goodbye,
she stepped into the carriage and rode off, her heart filled
with joy.

When Cinderella arrived at the palace, the ball was in full swing. She was welcomed with a fanfare of trumpets and she marvelled to see so many fine penguins wearing such magnificent costumes.

Her stepmother and stepsisters didn't notice her. They

were too busy gobbling down snacks and party sandwiches at the buffet tables.

But the Penguin Prince noticed Cinderella at once.

"Who is she?" he asked his courtiers. "She is the most beautiful penguin I have ever seen."

Cinderella had never met as handsome and charming a penguin as the Prince. From their first dance together he never left her side. They whirled and twirled around the dance floor to the applause of the admiring crowd.

"Who is the beautiful young penguin who has captured
the Prince's attention so completely?" everyone whispered.

"What a handsome couple! How well they dance
together!" they sighed.

Cinderella had never been so happy. She wished the night
could last forever.

Then, suddenly, she glanced up at the clock. In all the
excitement, she had completely forgotten the Fairy's warning.
"Oh!" she cried. "It's almost midnight. I have to go!"
And she ran from the palace in such a hurry that one of
her glass flippers fell off and was left lying on the steps.

As Cinderella rode away in her carriage, the Prince called out, "Oh, please don't go!"

But she was gone.

He picked up the glass flipper and said sadly, "Who was she? I don't even know her name."

The next day it was announced that the Prince would
marry the penguin whose foot fit the little glass flipper. There
was great excitement throughout the land. First, all the
princesses tried it on and then all the penguins of the court,
but the flipper was always too small.

The royal footmen were commanded to take the flipper
from house to house.

The stepsisters spent the whole day perfuming and powdering their feet.

"Cinderella," said the stepmother. "Your clothes are too ragged to be seen by the royal footmen. Go downstairs and polish the silver until they leave."

"Oh, please, I would like to try on the flipper, too!" said Cinderella, knowing it would fit her perfectly.

The stepsisters laughed, but then they looked down at Cinderella's webbed feet. For the first time they noticed how delicate they were.

A knock came at the front door.

"Quick! Hide her!" said the stepsisters.

They grabbed Cinderella, threw her down the cellar steps and slammed the door.

Poor Cinderella. She lay upside down with her foot caught tight in the door, unable to get free.

When the footmen came in, the stepsisters pushed and shoved to be first to try on the flipper. They were so intent on snatching the flipper from each other that it slipped from their grasp, flipped high in the air, and landed squarely on Cinderella's foot!

Everyone stared. It was a perfect fit.

As the footmen opened the door and helped Cinderella up, the Great Fairy Penguin appeared. With a tap of her magic wand, she transformed Cinderella's tattered rags into the magnificent clothes she had worn to the ball.

Cinderella was overjoyed. "Oh thank you, Fairy Penguin! I thank you with all my heart!"

The stepmother's and stepsisters' beaks dropped wide open. They stared at Cinderella, spluttering with amazement.

"Look! Oh my!"

"It's her! Oh no!"

"Oh dear! We've really put our foot in it!"

The Penguin Prince and Cinderella Penguin were married the very next day, and the wedding bells rang throughout the land. Never before could anyone remember such a joyous and happy wedding.

Cinderella and the Prince truly loved each other and they
lived happily together ever after.